Please return/renew this item by the last date shown
on this label, or on your self-service receipt.

To renew this item, visit **www.librarieswest.org.uk**
or contact your library.

Your Borrower number and PIN are required.

Libraries**West**

THE TRAVELLING COMPANION

For Ronald Hastie a part-time job in Paris' legendary Shakespeare and Company bookstore is the perfect way to spend a summer before he returns to Edinburgh to begin his PhD on Robert Louis Stevenson.

But when he meets a collector who claims to have the original manuscripts of both the first draft of Dr. Jekyll and Mr. Hyde and the never-published *The Travelling Companion* – both thought to have been destroyed by the author – a reckless obsession stirs inside him.

Ian Rankin is the bestselling author of the Inspector Rebus and Detective Malcom Fox novels. His books have been translated into thirty-six languages. He is the recipient of four CWA Dagger Awards and an Edgar Award.

IAN RANKIN

THE TRAVELLING
COMPANION

First published in the United States of America in
2016 by The Mysterious Bookshop, LLC

This edition first published in the UK in 2016 by
Head of Zeus Ltd

9 7 5 3 1 2 4 6 8

ISBN (HB) 9781786690661
ISBN (E) 9781784979997

A catalogue record for this book is available from
the British Library.

Typeset by Adrian McLaughlin
Printed and bound in the UK by Clays Ltd, St Ives Plc

Head of Zeus Ltd
Clerkenwell House
45–47 Clerkenwell Green
London EC1R 0HT
WWW.HEADOFZEUS.COM

THE TRAVELLING
COMPANION

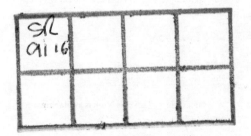

him a favour. How could I refuse?

I watched as my fingers plucked the postcard from his grip. It was one of the bookstore's own promotional cards. On one side were drawings of Shakespeare and Rue de la Bûcherie, on the other my handwritten destination.

'A five-minute walk,' Mr Whitman assured me. His accent was an American drawl. He was tall, his silver hair swept back from his forehead, his eyes deep-set, cheekbones prominent. The first time we'd met, he had demanded a cigarette. On hearing that I didn't smoke, he had shaken his head as if in general weariness at my generation. This meeting had taken place outside a nearby cous-cous restaurant, where I had been staring at the menu in the window, wondering if I dared go inside. Money wasn't the main issue. I had been rehearsing my few French phrases and considering the possibility that the staff, seeing me for a lone traveller, might mug me for my pocketful of francs before selling the contents of my heavy rucksack at some street market in the vicinity.

'Passing through?' the stranger next to me had inquired, before demanding that I give him one of my 'smokes'.

A little later, as we shared a table and the menu's cheapest options, he had told me about his bookstore.

'I know it,' I'd stammered. 'It's rightly famous.'

He had offered a tired smile, and, when we'd filled our bellies, had produced an empty thermos flask, into which he poured the leftover food before screwing the lid back on.

'No point wasting it,' he had explained. 'The store doesn't pay, you know, but there's the offer of a bed. A bed's all you get.'

'I was going to look for a hotel.'

'You work the till for a few hours, and mop the floor at closing time. Rest of the day's your own, and we do have some interesting books on the shelves...'

Which is how I came to work at Shakespeare and Company, 37 Rue de la Bûcherie, Paris 5. On the postcard we boasted 'the largest stock of antiquarian English books on the continent', and added Henry Miller's comment that we were 'a wonderland of books'.

It wasn't the original shop, of course – not that we trumpeted the fact. Sylvia Beach's Shakespeare and Company had opened in the year 1919 on Rue Dupuytren, before moving to larger premises on Rue de l'Odéon. This was where Joyce, Pound and Hemingway could be found. Mr Whitman had called his own bookstore Le Mistral, before renaming it in Beach's honour – her own Shakespeare and Co.

having closed for good during the German occupation of Paris. The new Shakespeare and Company had been a magnet for Beat writers in the 1950s, and writers (of a sort) still visited. I would lie on my hard narrow bed in a curtained-off alcove and listen as poems were workshopped by ex-pats whose names meant nothing to me. Contemporary writing was not my period, however, so I tried hard not to judge.

'You're from Scotland, right?' Mr Whitman had said to me one day.

'Edinburgh, specifically.'

'Walter Scott and Robbie Burns, eh?'

'And Robert Louis Stevenson.'

'Not forgetting that reprobate Trocchi...' He had chuckled to himself.

'Stevenson is my passion. I'm starting my PhD on him in the autumn.'

'Back into academe so soon?'

'I like it there.'

'I can't imagine why.' And he had fixed me with one of his looks, before opening the till to examine the evening's scant takings. It was August, and still hot outside. The tourists were sitting at café tables, fanning themselves with menus and ordering cold drinks. Only one or two people my own age were browsing the shelves of our airless shop. There was an original copy of *Ulysses* in the window, a siren to draw them inside. But this night it was proving ineffectual.

'Was Paris always your destination?' he asked, sliding the drawer closed again.

'I wanted to travel. Stevenson visited France several times.'

'Is that the subject of your PhD?'

'I'm looking at how his health may have affected his writing.'

'Sounds fascinating. But it's hardly living,

is it?' I watched him as he turned away and headed for the stairs. Three more hours and I could lock up before heading for bed and the various biting insects who seemed to feast nightly on my ankles and the backs of my knees.

I had sent postcards – Shakespeare and Company postcards – to friends and family, making sure to add a few centimes to the till in payment. I didn't mention the bites, but did make sure that my ongoing adventure sounded as exotic as possible. I had actually sent a first postcard home soon after disembarking from the overnight bus at London's Victoria Coach Station. Another had been purchased and sent from the ferry terminal in Dover. I knew my parents would prefer written communication to an expensive phone call. My father was a Church of Scotland minister, my mother an invaluable member of our local community.

I was a rarity of sorts in having stayed at home during the four years of my undergraduate degree. My parents had offered financial assistance towards rent, but my arguments about wasted money had swayed them. Besides, my childhood bedroom suited me, and my mother was the finest cook in the city.

Before leaving, however, I had promised to phone Charlotte every two days, just so she would know I was safe. There was a public phonebox just along the Seine from the store, with a view towards Notre-Dame which made up for its general lack of hygiene. With the receiver wrapped in a clean paper serviette from a café, I would spend a few francs telling Charlotte of any new experiences, in between listening to her tell me that she loved me and missed me and couldn't wait until I found a place of my own in time for the start of term back in Edinburgh.

'Absolutely,' I would agree, my mouth suddenly dry.

'Oh, Ronnie,' she would sigh, and I would swallow back the inclination to correct her, since my preference (as she well knew) was for Ronald rather than Ronnie.

My name is Ronald Hastie. I was born in 1960, making me twenty-two. Twenty-two and three months as I stood on the banks of the Seine, surrounded by heat and traffic fumes and a sense that there was another world being kept hidden from me. A series of worlds, actually, only one of them represented by Charlotte and her cropped red hair and freckled complexion. Cous-cous and a famous bookshop and morning espressos (consumed standing at the bar – the cheapest option) – these were all wonders to me that summer. And, yes, the original plan had been to drift much further south, but plans could change, as could people.

'The seller's English,' my employer said, waking me from my reverie. 'You'll be fine, trust me. A five-minute walk…'

His name was Benjamin Turk and he lived in a sprawling apartment at the top of five winding flights of stairs. When he opened his door to me, I stood there breathless, staring past him at a long hallway filled with groaning book-shelves. I felt light-headed, and it seemed in that moment that the shelves were endless, stretching to infinity. Turk slid an arm around my shoulders and guided me into the gloom.

'Whitman sent you but he didn't men-tion the climb. That's the reason he wouldn't drag his own sorry rump over here, you know.' Laughter boomed from his chest. He was stocky and bald and probably in his fifties or early sixties, with dark bushy eyebrows above eyes filled with sly humour. His voluminous white shirt and crimson waistcoat could have come from a different century, as could their owner. I'd read enough Dickens to see that Mr Turk would have slotted right into one of those comedic episodes from *Copperfield* or *Pickwick*.

'A drink's what's needed,' he went on, steering me down the hall. Varnished parquet floor stretched its length, and it ended eventually at a wall furnished with a large mirror, in which I glimpsed my sweating face. Doorways to left and right, both open, showing a tidy kitchen and a cluttered living-room. We entered this last and Turk positioned me before an armchair, thumping it so hard dust rose into the air.

'Sit!' he commanded, before pouring red wine from a glass decanter. I noticed for the first time that he had a discernible limp.

'I don't really...' I began to apologise.

'Nonsense, lad! This is Paris – you do realise that? Get it down you or I'll have you deported for crimes against the state!'

He had poured himself a glass not quite as generous as mine, and raised his hand in a toast before filling his mouth.

I realised I really was thirsty, so took a sip. The stuff was nectar, unlike the cheap, weak compromises of Edinburgh lunches and dinners. Cherries and blackcurrants replaced the bitter memories, and Turk could tell I was in love. He beamed at me, nodding slowly.

'Delicious,' I said.

'Did you ever doubt it?' And he toasted me again with his glass before settling on the chaise longue opposite. 'Do I detect a Scottish accent?'

'Edinburgh.'

'That most Presbyterian of cities, explaining your aversion to pleasure.'

'I'm not averse to pleasure.' As soon as the words were out, I regretted them, hoping they wouldn't be misinterpreted. To cover my embarrassment, I took more sips of wine, causing Turk to spring to his feet in order to refill my glass.

'Mr Whitman says you're one of his oldest customers,' I stammered.

'We've known one another more years than I care to remember.'

'So you've lived in Paris a long time?'

He smiled, this time a little wistfully. 'How about you?' he asked.

'This is my first visit. I'm taking a break from university.'

'Yes, George said as much – too short a break, he seems to think. Your hero Stevenson didn't let college hold him back, did he?' He saw my surprise. 'George again,' he explained.

'Stevenson completed his studies.'

'And passed the law exam,' Turk said airily. 'But his family expected him to stick to that path, or one very like it, but the bold Louis had other ideas.' My host was swirling the wine in his glass. I found the motion hypnotic, and sensed I was not yet fully recovered from the climb. The room was stuffy, too, with the smell of leatherbound books, old curtains and faded rugs.

'You should take your jacket off,' Turk said. 'Who the hell wears a black velvet jacket in Paris in the heat of summer?'

'It's not velvet,' I mumbled, shrugging my arms out of the sleeves.

'But the nearest you could find?' Turk smiled to himself and I could tell that he knew – knew that Stevenson's nickname at university had been 'Velvet Jacket'.

I lay the jacket across my knees and cleared

my throat. 'Mr Whitman says you have some books to sell.'

'A few boxes – mostly bought from George himself. He says you've memorised the stock so will know if they're worth taking or not.'

'He's exaggerating.'

'I think so, too. I know only too well how many books are in that shop of his.'

'You're a collector.' I was looking around the room. Every inch of wall-space was filled with shelving, and those shelves groaned. The books all seemed very old – few had dust jackets. It was impossible to make out any of the titles, but they seemed to be in several languages. 'Are you a professor? A writer?'

'I've been many things.' He paused, watching me above the rim of his glass. 'I'm guessing you'd like to be both some day.'

'I've never thought about writing. I mean to say, I would hope to finish my thesis and try to get it published.'

'A thesis about Stevenson and his ailments?'

'And how they made him the writer he was. He was trying out an experimental drug called ergotine when he got the idea for *Jekyll and Hyde*. It gave him hallucinations. And the Edinburgh he grew up in was all science and rationalism and men who *did* things, while he felt sickly, his only real strength his imagination...' I broke off, fearing I was beginning to lecture my host.

'Interesting,' Turk said, drawing the word out. He rose to fill my glass again, emptying the decanter. My mouth felt furred and sweat was trickling down my forehead. I took out a handkerchief and began to mop at my face. 'He had a nursemaid, didn't he?' Turk asked as he poured. 'She told him ghost stories. Must have frightened the life out of him.'

'He called her "Cummy" – her real name

was Alison Cunningham. She told him about the wardrobe in his room.'

'The one made by William Brodie?'

And Turk nodded to himself again, because he knew this story too. Brodie, a respectable man by day but a criminal by night, the Deacon of Wrights who led a gang, breaking into houses, thieving and terrorising, until caught, tried and hanged on a gibbet he had previously crafted by his own hand. The lazy theory was that Stevenson had plundered this story wholesale for *Jekyll and Hyde*, but it comprised only one part of the overall puzzle.

'Maybe we should look at these books,' I said, hoping I wasn't slurring my words.

'Of course.' Turk rose slowly to his feet, and came over to help me up. I followed him into the kitchen. There was a narrow stairway I hadn't noticed and we climbed into the eaves of the building. It was hotter, gloomier and stuffier up here. Two people, no matter how emaciated, could not have passed one another in the corridor. Several doors led off. One seemed to be a bathroom. I guessed there had to be a bedroom, but the room Turk led me into was the study. Three boxes sat on an antique desk. Piles of books lined the walls, threatening to topple as our weight shifted the bare floorboards beneath. I draped my jacket over the room's only chair.

'Shall I leave you to it, then?' Turk inquired.

I looked in vain for a window to open. The sweat was stinging my eyes now and my handkerchief was drenched. Outside, bells were chiming. The scratching noises could have been pigeons on the roof-tiles immediately overhead or rats somewhere below the floor. My lips felt as if they had been glued together. More dust flew into my face as I peeled open the flaps of the first box.

'You don't look well, my boy.' Turk's words seemed to come from far off. Were we still in the attic, or had we somehow moved to that infinite entrance-hall with its books and mirror? I had a sudden vision: a cold drink, something non-alcoholic, in a tall glass filled with ice. I craved it without being able to say the words out loud. There was a book in my hand, but it seemed to weigh far more than its size would suggest, and the title on its spine seemed to be a jumble of letters or hieroglyphs of some kind.

'My boy?'

And then a darkening tunnel.

'Wait, let me…'

And then sleep.

I awoke laid out on a bed. My shirt had been unbuttoned and Benjamin Turk was dabbing at my chest with a damp towel. I sat bolt upright, a hangover pulsing behind my eyes.

It was quite obviously *his* bedroom. My jacket had been placed on a hook on the back of the door, but below it I could see a long red satin bath-robe. There was also a wardrobe whose doors wouldn't quite shut and a bedside table bearing a basin half-filled with water. When I angled my feet off the bed on to the floor, I made contact with several hardcover books lying there.

'Careful you don't faint again,' Turk cautioned as I started to rebutton my shirt.

'I just need some air,' I muttered.

'Of course. Can I help you negotiate the stairs?'

'I'll be fine.'

'I'm relieved to hear it – I had the devil's own job bringing you this far…'

I wasn't sure what he meant until I grabbed my jacket and pulled open the door. We were just inside the front door of the apartment. I must have missed the bedroom on arrival. I stared at Turk, who shrugged.

'It wasn't easy – those steps from the attic are treacherous.' He was holding something out for me to take. I unfolded the piece of paper. 'A list of the books,' he explained, 'so that your employer can be kept in blissful ignorance – if that's what you would like.'

'Thank you,' I said, pocketing the note. He had unlocked the door. The stairwell was a few degrees cooler, but I could still feel sweat clinging to my hair.

'Safe descent,' Benjamin Turk said, giving a little wave of one hand before disappearing behind the closing door. Holding on to the banister, I made my way slowly to the street, pausing outside and filling my lungs with air. A young woman on the pavement opposite seemed to be watching me. She wore a full-length floral-print dress, almost identical to one Charlotte owned. I did a double-take and my jacket slid to the ground. By the time I'd picked it up, she had gone. I began walking back to the shop, aware that my headache was going nowhere. Passing a bar, I headed in and ordered a Perrier with plenty of ice and lemon. Having finished it in two long draughts, I ordered another. I doubted the place would sell painkillers, but then remembered the old saying about the hair of the dog. Kill or cure, I thought to myself, adding a glass of red wine to my order.

And it worked – I could feel the pain easing after just one small measure. It was thin, vinegary stuff, too, the very antithesis of the contents of Turk's decanter, but I felt better for it, and ordered one final glass. While sipping this, I removed the list of books from my pocket and went through it. A solid line had been drawn across the sheet two-thirds of the way down. Underneath was a message from Turk:

Not for sale, but possibly of interest:
The Travelling Companion

I blinked a few times and furrowed my brow. I knew that title, but couldn't immediately place it. The books listed above it could probably find buyers. Historical non-fiction and philosophy titles mostly, with Balzac, Zola and Mann thrown in. Turk omitted to say whether they were first editions, or what condition they were in, and I had only the most fleeting memory of opening the first box. I felt I had let Mr Whitman down somehow – not that he need ever know, unless Turk decided to tell him. But that didn't stop me feeling bad. Preoccupied, I was halfway to the doorway before the barman reminded me I hadn't yet paid. I mumbled an apology and rooted in my pockets for change. Curiously, there seemed a couple of hundred-franc notes there that I thought I'd spent earlier in the week. There would be cous-cous again that evening, rather than a tin of cheap tuna from the supermarket. Heartened, I added a small tip to the bill.

An Australian backpacker called Mike was minding the store on my return. He told me, to my relief, that Mr Whitman would be gone the rest of the day. I resented Mike his broad-shouldered height, perfect teeth and mahogany tan. His hair was blond and curly and he had already made his mark on a couple of female students who liked to hang about the place, reading but never buying. When he ended his shift and I took over, I found that there was a letter for me next to the till. Typical of him not to have mentioned it. It was from my father and I opened it as respectfully as possible. Two small sheets of thin blue airmail. He had news of my mother, my aunt and uncle, my clever cousins – clever in that they both had good jobs in the City of London – and the neighbours on our street. His tone was clipped and precise, much like his sermons, not a word wasted. My mother had added a couple of lines towards the foot of the last page, but seemed to feel that nothing really need be added to my father's update. The return address had been added to the back of the envelope, lest it be lost in transit somehow. As I reread it, I caught a glimpse of someone on the pavement outside, someone wearing the same floral dress as before. I sauntered to the open doorway and looked up and down the street, but she had done her vanishing act again – if it had been her in the first place. What I did see, however, a third time. The house wine was thinner than anything I had yet tasted, but I nodded my appreciation of it when invited to do so by my waiter. And at the meal's end, this same waiter, who had told me a couple of visits back to call him Harry, signalled that he would meet me at the restaurant's kitchen door in five minutes. Having paid the bill, my curiosity piqued, I wound my way down the alley behind the restaurant and its neighbours. The bins were overflowing and there was a strong smell of urine. I skidded once or twice, not daring to look down at whatever was beneath my feet. Eventually I reached Harry. He stood at the open door of the kitchen while vocal mayhem ensued within, accompanied by the clanging of cooking-pots. He was holding a thin cigarette, which he proceeded to light, sucking deeply on it before offering it to me.

'Dope?' I said.

'Very good.'

After four years of an arts degree at the University of Edinburgh, I was no stranger to drugs. I had been to several parties where a room – usually an underlit bedroom – had been set aside for use by drug-takers. I'd even watched as joints were rolled, enjoying the ritual while refusing to partake.

'I'm not sure,' I told Harry, whose real name was more like Ahmed. 'It's been a strange enough day already.' When he persisted, however, I lifted the cigarette from him and took a couple of puffs without inhaling. This wasn't good enough for Harry, who used further gestures to instruct me until he was happy that I had sucked the smoke deep into my lungs. Another waiter joined us and it was soon his turn. Then Harry. Then me again. I had expected to feel queasy, but that didn't happen. My cares seemed to melt away, or at least take on a manageable perspective. Once we had finished the joint, Harry produced a small cellophane wrap, inside which was a lump of something brown. He wanted two hundred francs for it, but I shrugged to signal that I didn't have that kind of money about my person. So then he shoved the tiny parcel into my jacket pocket and patted it, gesturing to indicate that I could pay him later.

We then fell silent as two new arrivals entered the alley. They either hadn't noticed that they had an audience, or else they simply weren't bothered. The woman squatted in front of the man and unzipped his trousers. I had seen more than a few prostitutes on my night-time walks through the city – some of whom had tried tempting me – and here was another, hard at work while the woozy client tipped a bottle of vodka to his mouth.

And suddenly I knew.

The Travelling Companion…

I lifted a hand to my forehead with the shock of it, while my companions took a step back towards their kitchen, perhaps fearing I was about to be sick.

'No,' I whispered to myself. 'That can't be right.' Harry was looking at me, and I returned his stare. 'It doesn't exist,' I told him. 'It doesn't exist.'

Having said which, I weaved my way back towards the mouth of the alley, almost stumbling into the woman and her client. He swore at me, and I swore back, almost pausing to take a swing at him. It wasn't the alcohol or the dope making my head reel as I sought the relative calm of the darkened Shakespeare and Company.

It was Benjamin Turk's message to me…

I was unlocking the doors next morning when

Mr Whitman called down to tell me I had a phone call.

'And by the way, how did you get on with Ben Turk?'

'I have a note of the books he wants to sell,' I replied, not meeting his eyes.

'He's an interesting character. Anyway, go talk to your woman friend…'

It was Charlotte. She had found work at a theatre box office and was using their phone.

'I need to pass the time somehow. It's so *boring* here without you.'

I was leaning down to rub at the fresh insect-bites above my ankles. The list from Turk was folded up in the back pocket of my trousers. I knew I had to tear a strip from it before showing it to my employer.

'Are you there?' Charlotte was asking into the silence.

'I'm here.'

'Is everything okay? You sound…'

'I'm fine. A glass of wine too many last night.'

I heard her laugh. 'Paris is leading you astray.'

'Maybe just a little.'

'Well, that can be a good thing.' She paused. 'You remember our little chat, the night before you left?'

'Yes.'

'I meant it, you know. I'm ready to take things a bit further. *More* than ready.'

She meant sex. Until now, we had kissed, and gone from fumbling above clothes to rummaging beneath them, but nothing more.

'It's what you want, too, isn't it?' she asked.

'Doesn't everyone?' I was able to answer, my cheeks colouring.

'So when you come back… we'll do something about it, yes?'

'If you're sure. I mean, I don't want to push you into anything.'

More laughter. 'I seem to be the one doing the pushing. I'm thinking of you right now, you know. Thinking of *us* lying together, joined together – tell me you don't think about that, too.'

'I have to go, Charlotte. There are customers…' I looked around the empty upstairs room.

'Soon, Ronnie, soon. Just remember.'

'I will. I'll call you tonight.'

I put the phone down and stared at it, then took the note from my pocket and tore across it. Downstairs, my employer was manning the till.

'You look like hell, by the way,' he said as I handed him the list. 'Did Ben ply you with booze?'

'Do you know much about him?'

'He comes from money. Pitched up here

for want of anywhere better – not unlike my good self. Drinks fine wines, buys books he wants to own but not necessarily read.' He was scanning the list. 'He'd probably give these to us for free, you know. I think he just needs space for more of the same.' He paused, fixing me with a look. 'What did *you* think of him?'

'Pleasant enough. Maybe a bit eccentric…' I suppressed a shiver as I remembered waking on Turk's bed, shirt open, and him dabbing at my chest. 'Is he…' I tried to think how to phrase the question. 'A ladies' man?'

Mr Whitman hooted. 'Listen to you,' he said. 'Remind me – which century is this?' After his laughter had subsided, he fixed his eyes on mine again. 'Ladies, gents, fish and fowl and the beasts of field and wood,' he said. 'Now off you go and find yourself some breakfast. I'll manage these heaving crowds somehow.' He waved his arm in the direction of the deserted shop.

It was warm outside, and noisy with tourists and traffic. I slung my jacket over my shoulder as I walked to my usual café, only four shop-fronts away. Benjamin Turk was seated at an outdoor table, finishing a *café au lait* and reading *Le Monde*. A silver-topped walking-stick rested against the rim of the table. He gestured for me to join him, so I dragged out the spare metal chair and sat down, slipping my jacket over the back of my chair.

'It was the local prostitutes who called Stevenson "Velvet Jacket", you know,' Turk said.

The liveried waiter stood ready. I ordered a coffee of my own.

'And an orange juice,' Turk added.

The waiter gave a little bow and headed back inside. Turk folded the newspaper and laid it next to his cup.

'I was coming to check on you,' he said. 'But the lure of caffeine was too strong.'

'I'm fine,' I assured him.

'And you've looked at the list, I presume?'

I took the scrap of paper from my pocket and placed it between us. He gave an indulgent smile.

'It's a book Stevenson wrote,' I said. 'Never quite completed. His publisher liked it well enough but considered the contents too sordid.'

'It concerned a prostitute,' Turk agreed.

'Set in Italy, I think.'

'Some of it.' Turk's eyes were gleaming.

'Fanny made Stevenson put it on the fire,' I said quietly.

'Ah, the formidable Fanny Osbourne. He met her in France, you know. He was visiting Grez. I suppose he became infatuated.'

He paused, playing with his cup, moving it in circles around its saucer. 'It wasn't the only book of his she persuaded him to sacrifice…'

'*Jekyll and Hyde*,' I said, as my own coffee arrived, and with it the glass of juice. 'The first draft, written in three days.'

'Yes.'

'Though some commentators say three days is impossible.'

'Despite the author's Presbyterian work ethic. But then he was taking drugs, wasn't he?'

'Ergotine, and possibly cocaine.'

'Quite the cocktail for a writer whose imagination was already inflamed. You know why he consigned it to the flames?'

'Fanny persuaded him. She thought it would ruin his reputation.'

'Because it was too raw, too shocking.' He watched me as I finished the orange juice in two long gulps, watched as I poured hot milk into the viscous black coffee.

'Nobody really knows, though,' I eventually said. 'Because only Stevenson and Fanny saw that first version. Same goes for *The Travelling Companion*.'

'Not quite.'

'Yes, his publisher read that,' I corrected myself.

'Not quite,' Turk repeated, almost in a whisper.

'You're not seriously telling me you have that manuscript?'

'Do you really think any author could burn the only copy of a work they considered worthwhile?'

'Didn't Fanny see it burn in the grate?'

'She saw *something* burn. She saw paper. I'm guessing there would have been plenty of paper in the vicinity.'

Lifting the coffee towards my mouth, I realised my hand was shaking. He waited until I'd taken a first sip.

'I have *both* manuscripts,' he then announced, causing me to splutter. I rubbed the back of my hand across my lips.

'I'm not sure I believe you,' I eventually said.

'Why not?'

'Because they'd be worth a small fortune. Besides, the world would know. It's been almost a century – impossible to have kept them a secret.'

'Nothing is impossible.'

'Then you'll show me them?'

'It can be arranged. But tell me – what would it mean for your doctoral thesis?'

I thought for a moment. 'They'd probably move me from student to full professor.' I laughed at the absurdity of it. Yet I almost believed... almost.

'My understanding,' Turk went on airily, 'is that he entrusted both to his good friend Henley. They found their way into my family because my grandfather bought many of Henley's possessions on his death – they were friends of a sort. There are notations in what seems to be Henley's handwriting. They add… well, you'd need to read them to find out.'

That smile again. I wanted to grab him and shake him.

'I'm not very good at keeping secrets,' I told him.

'Maybe it's time for the truth to be told,' he retorted. 'Wouldn't you say you're as good a vessel as any?' He had taken some coins from his pocket and was counting them on to the table top as payment for the drinks. 'I should imagine most Stevenson scholars would be on their knees right now, begging to be shown even a few pages.' He paused, reaching into his jacket. 'Pages like these.'

He held them out towards me. Half a dozen sheets.

'Copies rather than the originals, you understand.'

Handwritten on unlined paper.

'The openings to both books,' Turk was saying as my head swam and my eyes strained to retain their focus. 'You'll notice something from the off…'

'Edinburgh,' I mouthed, near-silently.

'The setting for both,' he agreed. 'Well, there *are* some French scenes in *The Travelling Companion*, but our harlot heroine hails from your own fair city, Ronald. And since Jekyll is reputed to be a conflation between Deacon Brodie and the Scottish physician John Hunter, I suppose Edinburgh makes sense – too much sense for Fanny to bear, as it transpired.'

I glanced up at him, seeking his meaning.

'There's too much of Stevenson himself in both works,' he obliged, rising to his feet.

'You could be the victim of a hoax,' I blurted out. 'I mean to say, forgeries maybe.' I held the pages up in front of me, my heart racing.

'Handwriting analysis comes later on in the story,' Turk said, adjusting the cuffs of his pale linen jacket and seeming to sniff the mid-morning air. 'I expect you'll be paying me a visit later – if only to collect those boxes of books.'

'This is insane,' I managed to say, holding the pages by both trembling hands.

'Nevertheless, you'll want to read them. I'm out most of the day, but should be home later this evening.'

He turned and walked away, leaning lightly on his walking-stick. I watched him. He seemed to belong to a different age or culture. It was something about his gait as well as his clothes.

I could imagine him with a top hat propped on his head, horse-drawn carriages passing him as he tip-tapped his way down the boulevard. The waiter said '*merci*' as he scooped up the coins and cleared the table, but I was in no rush to leave. I read and reread the excerpts. They revealed little by way of plot, but it was true that Edinburgh was the setting for both, Stevenson's descriptions of his 'precipitous city' as trenchant as ever. It was a place he seemed to have loved and hated in equal measure. I recalled something I'd read about his student years – how he spent his time yoyoing between the strict rationalism of the family home in Heriot Row and the drunken stews of the chaotic Old Town – moving, in other words, between the worlds of Henry Jekyll and Edward Hyde.

When the waiter cleared his throat, alerting me to the fact my premium table was needed by a wealthy American couple, I rolled the sheets of paper into a tube and carried them back to the shop. My employer had ceded his place behind the till to a new arrival, an English woman called Tessa with long brown hair, round glasses, and a prominent nose.

'I'll be upstairs if you need me,' I told her. The curtain had been drawn closed across my alcove. Pulling it back revealed Mike and one of his female friends, both naked from the waist up and sharing slugs from a cheap bottle of wine. The young woman apologised in French-accented English and slipped a T-shirt over her head.

'Ronnie doesn't mind a bit of tit,' Mike told her with a grin. She punched his arm and snatched the bottle from him, offering it to me. I settled on the corner of the bed and took a mouthful.

'What's that you've got?' Mike asked.

'Nothing important,' I lied, stuffing the sheets of paper into my jacket pocket. There was something else in there, and I fished it out. It was the lump of dope.

'That what I think it is?' Mike said, his grin widening. 'Well, now we've got us a proper party!' He leapt up, returning a minute or two later with everything he needed. Cross-legged, he began to assemble the joint. 'You're a dark horse, mate,' he told me. 'Never would have thought you indulged.'

'Then you don't know me very well.' His friend had moved closer, her leg touching mine. I could make out the soft down on her face. When she passed me the lit joint, it was as intimate as any kiss.

'It's not the best I've had,' Mike said, when his turn came. 'But it'll do, *n'est-ce pas, chérie*?'

'It'll do,' his friend echoed.

It was not ergotine, nor yet cocaine, but

I found my imagination heightened. I was with Stevenson and his student allies, touring the taverns of Edinburgh, rubbing shoulders with slatterns and sophisticates. I was adrift in France, and sailing to Samoa, and roughing it in Silverado, having survived yet another near-fatal illness. I was weak in body but strong in spirit, and a woman loved me. I was writing *Jekyll and Hyde* as an exorcism of sorts, my demons vanquished, allowing me the less dangerous pleasures of *Kidnapped* less than a year later. External as well as internal adventures were my mainstay – I had to keep moving, ever further from the Edinburgh of my birth and formation. I had to remake myself, renew myself, heal myself, even as mortality drew close. I had to survive.

'What's that?' Mike asked. He was slumped on the bed with his head against the wall.

'I didn't say anything.'

'Something about survival.'

'No.'

He turned to his friend. She had moved next to him so that only her bare unwashed feet now rested near me. 'You heard him,' he nudged her.

'Survival,' she echoed.

'What it's all about,' Mike agreed, nodding slowly, before pulling himself together, the better to roll another joint.

Though I was stoned, I agreed to take over from Tessa while she headed out for food. Mike and Maryse – she had eventually told me her name – decided to go with her. They had the decency to ask if I wanted anything, but I shook my head. I gulped some water from the tap and took up position. A few customers came and went. One or two regulars got comfortable with books they would never buy. Later, a writing group would hold its weekly meeting upstairs. And there she was again. Not just a glimpse this time, but a solidity in the open doorway, in the same floral dress. A willowy figure topped with long blonde hair. Her eyes were on mine, but when I signalled for her to approach, she shook her head, so I walked towards her.

'I've seen you before,' I said.

'You're Ronald,' she stated.

'How do you know my name?'

'Ben told me.'

'You know Benjamin Turk?'

She nodded slowly. 'You mustn't trust him. He likes playing games with people.'

'I've only met him twice.'

'Yet he's already got beneath your skin – don't try to deny it.'

'Who *are* you?'

'I'm Alice.'

'How do you know Mr Turk?'

'Services rendered.'

'I'm not sure I follow.'

'I run errands for him sometimes. I copied those pages he gave you.'

'You know about those?'

'You've already read them, I suppose?'

'Of course.'

'And you need to read more, meaning you'll visit him again?'

'I think so.'

She had lifted her hand and was running the tips of her fingers down my cheek, as if human contact was something new and strange. I leaned back a little, but she took a step forward and pressed her lips against mine, kissing me, her eyes squeezed shut. When she opened them again, I sensed a vast lake of sadness behind them. Tears were forming as she turned and fled down the street. I stood like a statue, shocked to my very core, wondering if I should go after her, but one of the loiterers had decided to break the habit of a lifetime and pay for the book in his hands, so I shrugged off the incident and headed back to the till, not in the least surprised to find that the book being purchased was the copy of *Heart of Darkness* I'd taken with me to the cous-cous restaurant...

It was almost eleven by the time I found myself standing outside Benjamin Turk's building. I stared up towards the top floor. A few lights were burning, but I couldn't be sure which rooms were his. I pushed open the heavy door and began to climb the stairs. I could smell the aftermath of various dinners, and hear conversations – mostly, I guessed, from TV sets. There was a dog behind one door, scratching and complaining softly. Having reached the top floor, and while pausing to catch my breath, I saw a note pinned to Turk's door.

Still out. Come in.

I tried the door. It was unlocked. The overhead light was on in the hallway, but as with most Parisian lighting it seemed woefully underpowered. I called out but received no reply. There was something lying on the floor a few yards into the apartment – further sheets of manuscript, again photocopied. I lifted them and carried them into the living room, where I settled on the same chair as before. A fresh decanter of wine had been laid out, alongside two crystal glasses.

'In for a centime,' I muttered to myself, pouring some. Then, having rolled up my shirt-sleeves, I began to read.

The two extracts did not follow on from their predecessors. They were from deeper into both books. I soon saw why Turk had chosen them, however – both recounted very similar incidents, vicious attacks on women whose bodies were for sale. In *The Travelling Companion*, it was the courtesan of the title who was brutalised by an unnamed stranger while passing down one of the steep inclines off Edinburgh's High Street. In the version of *Jekyll and Hyde*, the victim's attacker was Edward Hyde. But Hyde's name had replaced another, scored through in ink until it was all but obliterated. Pencilled marginalia, however, indicated that the name Stevenson had originally chosen for his monster was Edwin Hythe. Indeed, the margins of this particular page were filled with notes and comments in various hands – Stevenson's, I felt sure, but maybe also his friend Henley's – and Fanny's, too? Was it she who had written in blunt capital letters 'NOT HYTHE!'?

I poured myself some more wine and

began deciphering the scribbles, scrawls and amendments. I was still hard at work when I heard the door at the end of the hallway open and close, footsteps drawing close. Then Benjamin Turk was standing there in the doorway, coat draped over both shoulders. He was dressed to the nines, and had obviously enjoyed his evening, his face filled with colour, eyes almost fiery.

'Ah, my dear young friend,' he said, shrugging off the coat and resting his walking-stick against a pile of books.

'I hope you don't mind,' I replied, indicating the decanter.

He landed heavily in the chair opposite, his girth straining the buttons on his shirt. 'Do you still imagine you're in the presence of a cruel hoax?' he asked, exhaling noisily.

'Not so much, perhaps.'

This caused him to smile, albeit tiredly.

'Do we know who wrote the notes in the margins?'

'The usual suspects.' He rose long enough to pour some wine. 'Edwin Hythe,' he drawled.

'Yes.'

'You won't know who he is?' Settling himself, he studied me over the rim of his glass.

'He's Hyde.'

But Turk shook his head slowly. 'He was a friend of Stevenson's, one of the students he drank with back in the day.'

'That was his real name? And Stevenson was going to use it in the book?' I sounded sceptical because I was.

'I know.' Turk took a sip, savouring the wine. 'Hythe had re-entered Stevenson's life, visiting him in Bournemouth not long before work started on the story you're holding. The two had fallen out at some point and not spoken for several years. There are a couple of

portraits of Hythe – I've seen them but don't have copies to hand. I do have this though…'
He reached into his jacket and drew out a sheet of printed paper. I took it from him, unfolding it carefully. It was the front page of a newspaper of the time, the *Edinburgh Evening Courant*, from a February edition of 1870. The main story recounted the tale of a 'young woman known to the city's night-dwellers' who had been found 'most grievously slaughtered' in an alley off Cowgate.

'Like Stevenson,' Turk was saying, 'Edwin Hythe was a member of the university's Spec-ulative Society – though whatever speculation they did was accompanied by copious amounts of drink. And don't forget – this was at a time when Edinburgh was noted for scientific and medical experiments, meaning the students had access to pharmaceuticals of all kinds, most of them untested, a few probably lethal.

then rewrites the story, shifting location from Edinburgh to London and changing Hythe to Hyde...'

'Was he a doctor?'

'I'm sorry?'

I met Turk's look. 'Was Edwin Hythe a doctor?'

I watched him shake his head. I had emptied my glass and refilled it without thinking. 'How do you know all this?'

'It's a tale passed down through my family.'

'Why, though?'

'As a warning maybe.'

'You're a Hythe,' I stated, maintaining eye contact.

He eventually let out a snort of laughter. 'I sincerely hope not.' And he raised his own glass in a toast.

'Can I see the whole story?'

'Which one?'

'Both.'

'In good time.'

'Why not now?'

'Because I'm not sure you're ready.'

'I don't understand.'

But he just shook his head.

'It's like water torture,' I ploughed on. 'One page, two pages, three...'

'When I said that you weren't ready, I meant me – *I'm* not ready to let go, not just yet.'

'And after all these generations, why me?'

He offered a tired shrug. 'I'm the last of my line. Maybe that's reason enough. How about you?'

'Me?'

'Brothers...? Sisters...?'

'An only child.'

'We have that in common, too, then.' He yawned and stretched. 'Forgive me, I think I need some sleep.'

'I could stay here and read.'

He shook his head again. 'Perhaps tomorrow.' He rose to his feet and gestured for me to do the same. As he accompanied me down the hall, helping me into my jacket, I felt the negative mirror image of his fatigue. I was crackling with energy, a need to be in movement, a need for activity and exertion.

'I saw your friend,' I told him. 'She was passing the shop.'

'Oh?'

'Alice, with the blonde hair.'

'Alice,' he echoed.

'I just thought I'd say.'

'Thank you.' He pulled open the door and I skipped out, almost dancing down the stone stairs. She was waiting, of course – at the same spot across the street, wearing her floral dress and looking cold. I slipped off my jacket and placed it around her, then led her by the hand.

'Where are we going?' she asked.

'The river. I feel like walking.'

There were no tourist boats at this hour, just a few silent lovers and noisy drunks.

'Do you live with him?' I asked her.

'No.'

'So where do you live?'

'Not far.'

'Can we go there?'

'No.' She sounded almost aghast at the idea.

'My room back at the shop then,' I offered.

'Why would I go anywhere with you?'

'Because you kissed me.'

'I shouldn't have done that.'

'I'm glad you did though.' I came to a halt, facing her. 'I'd like it to happen again.'

She took a few moments to make her mind up, then stroked my face again, this time with both hands, as though checking that I really was flesh and blood. I leaned in and our lips met, mouths opening. But partway through, she started to laugh, easing away from me. I tried for a disappointed look, and she had the good grace to look slightly ashamed.

'I'm sorry,' she said. 'It's just…'

'What?'

'Nothing.' She shook her head, but then perked up and grabbed my hand, leading me along the riverfront towards the nearest brightly lit bridge. 'We can cross to the other side.'

'Why would we do that?'

'It's quieter there. Do you have any dope?'

'Just this.' I showed her the remains of the cannabis. 'I don't have any cigarettes or papers though.'

'That doesn't matter.' She peeled away the cellophane and nibbled at a corner. 'You can just eat it. It's almost nice.'

'Almost?' I smiled and bit into the gritty cube. 'Will it have the same effect?'

'We'll know the answer soon enough. Did Harry sell you this?'

'You know him?'

'If you've not paid, offer him half of whatever he asks.'

'What if he doesn't like that?'

She looked me up and down. 'You're bigger than him.'

'He has friends though.'

'So pull a knife.' She mimed the action of drawing a blade from its sheath and lunging with it. 'Straight into his gut and his friends will run for the hills.' She saw the look on my face and burst out laughing, hiding her mouth behind the palm of her hand. I grabbed both her arms and pulled her towards me, waiting until she was ready for our next kiss.

'Keep your eyes open this time,' I said in a whisper. 'I want to see whatever's in them…'

◆

For the next week, whenever I walked out of Shakespeare and Company, she was waiting. In deference to the dress she always wore, I'd stopped changing my own clothes, even though Mike had complained, wrinkling his nose as he made a show of sniffing my shoulder.

'Mate, when was the last time you saw the inside of a shower?'

But Alice didn't seem to mind. We would buy a plastic bottle of the cheapest wine and head for the river or the Louvre or the Arc de Triomphe, laughing at the tourists as they posed for their little photos. On one occasion, we indulged in a five-litre cubitainer of red, sharing it with the tramps who congregated near one of the bridges, until a fight broke out and the arrival of the *gendarmes* sent us scurrying. I had stopped shaving, and Alice would run her hands down my cheeks and across my chin, calling me her 'bit of rough'. There was a folded letter in my pocket from my father. I hadn't opened it, and hadn't troubled to call Charlotte. Theirs was another world entirely. I could feel myself changing, growing. When Harry grabbed me one night outside the restaurant to remind me of the money I owed, I laid him out with a single punch, after which I had to keep my distance from the restaurant. Not that this mattered – Alice never ate a thing, and that seemed to suit both of us. With money from the bookshop till, I bought us a few grams of cocaine from an African dealer, which killed any appetite remaining. And when Mike nagged me for missing a shift which he had been obliged to cover, I gave as good as I got, until he backed away, hands held in front of him, fear in his eyes at my clenched fists and gritted teeth.

Oh, yes, I was changing.

I'd been back to Benjamin Turk's apartment, but its door remained locked and unanswered. Alice had advised a shoulder-charge, which had left me with nothing other than a large bruise and a slight deflation of ego.

'I could scale the front wall, window to window,' I'd muttered over more pavement wine, receiving an indulgent smile and a hug.

'He's often gone for a few days,' she'd sympathised. 'He'll be back soon enough.'

And then she'd kissed me.

There hadn't been any sex as yet, which suited both of us. We were happy to wait for the right moment, the most intense moment. Hugs and kisses, the holding of hands, fingers stroking an arm, cheek or the nape of the neck. She seemed to have no other friends, or none she wouldn't give up in order to spend time with me, and I felt the same. I wasn't about to share what we had with Mike or anyone else. Every moment I could, I spent with her.

Until the day I walked downstairs into

the shop groggy with sleep and saw Charlotte standing there. She carried a rucksack and a wide-brimmed straw hat and looked hot from walking. Her smile was hesitant.

'Hello, you,' she said. 'We were getting worried.'

'Oh?'

'I phone but you're never here. And your mum and dad...' She broke off. 'Well, do I get a hug?'

I stepped forward and took her by the shoulders, my lips brushing against her damp red hair.

'Bloody hell, Ronnie, look at the state of you. When did you last eat?'

'I'm fine.'

'You're really not. Your friend Mike...'

'Mike?'

'He answered the phone yesterday.'

'And told you to come running? Probably

just wanted to size you up as another notch on his bed-post.'

'He was right though; you look ill. Have you seen a doctor?'

'I don't need a doctor. What I need is for everyone to stop bothering me.'

She was silent for a moment, glaring at me. Then she turned her eyes away. 'A lovely warm welcome for your girlfriend,' she muttered, pretending to study one of the shelves.

I ran a hand through my matted hair. 'Look, I had a bit to drink last night. And the shock of seeing you here…' I broke off. I'd been about to say that I was sorry, but part of me resisted. 'What time is it?'

'Nearly one.'

'I'll buy you something at the café.' I opened the till and lifted out a few notes.

'Is that allowed?' Charlotte asked as I stuffed the money into my pocket.

'I'll put it back later,' I lied.

When we stepped outside there was – for once – no sign of Alice, but Maryse was setting out boxes of cheap paperbacks on the pavement.

'Tell Mike I'll be having a word with him later,' I said, my face set like stone. Then I led Charlotte a few metres along the road, entering the café and taking up position by the counter. Charlotte slid the rucksack from her shoulders.

'Thinking of staying?' I inquired.

'I wasn't about to do Paris and back in a day. Since when did you smoke?'

I looked down at the cigarette I was rolling.

'Not sure,' I admitted. Which was the truth – I had no memory of buying either the pouch of Drum tobacco or the packet of tissue-thin papers. All I knew was that Alice obviously didn't mind. The look on Charlotte's face was properly small-minded and Presbyterian. I could imagine her sitting primly in my parents' drawing-room, holding cup and saucer and allowing herself 'one small slice of cake'. Home baking? Naturally. The conversation stilted and bourgeois and safe. Everything so fucking *safe*.

'What are you thinking?' she asked as I lit the slender cigarette.

'I'm thinking you shouldn't have come.'

Was she really becoming tearful, or merely putting on a show in the hope of sympathy? My espresso had arrived, along with her Perrier. The barman waved a bottle of red in my direction but I shook my head and he seemed to understand.

Pas devant les enfants…

'I wanted to see you,' Charlotte persisted. 'This is Paris, after all. Everyone says it's a romantic city and I've been missing you, Ronnie. I thought maybe this would be the place for us to…'

'What?'

She lowered her eyes and her voice. 'Don't make me say it.'

'Fuck our brains out?'

Her eyes and mouth widened. She glanced at the barman.

'He doesn't have any English,' I reassured her, knowing François would actually have understood every word. He was polishing glasses at the far end of the bar. All of a sudden I craved something alcoholic, so ordered a *pression*. When it arrived, I demolished it in two gulps, and nodded for a refill while Charlotte stared at me.

'You need help,' she eventually said. 'Something's happened to you.'

'Well, you're right about that at least – yes, something's happened to me. For the first time in my life, and I'm all the better for it.'

'You're not though. Look in the mirror.'

As it happened, there was a long narrow mirror running the length of the bar, below the row of optics and shelves of drinks. I hunched down so I could make eye contact with myself and couldn't help grinning.

'Who's that handsome devil?' I chuckled.

'Ronnie...'

'My name's Ronald!' I roared. François clucked and gestured for me to keep it down. I waved a hand in what could have passed for either apology or dismissal of his complaint.

Charlotte's hand was shaking as she lifted her glass of water. I realised that's what she was: carbonated water, while my life had become so much headier and filled with sensation.

'Will you help me find a hotel?' she was asking without making eye contact.

'Of course,' I said quietly.

'I'll change my flight to tomorrow, if I can. I was going to stay a few days, but...'

'They'll be missing you at your work.'

'Oh, I quit the job. My thinking was to do some travelling with you.' Finally she fixed her eyes on mine. 'But that was when you were you.'

'Who am I now?'

'I've really no idea.'

'Well, I'm sorry you had to come all this way to find out.' I placed a fifty-franc note on the counter and made to lift Charlotte's rucksack from the floor.

'No,' she snapped, hoisting it on to her shoulders. 'I can manage perfectly well.'

As we exited the café, I caught sight of a dress I recognised. Just the hem of it as its owner dodged around the corner of a building. We headed in the opposite direction, into the narrow maze of streets behind the bookshop. I looked behind me, but Alice didn't seem to be following. There were plenty of small hotels here, most of them doing good business at the height of the summer. It was twenty minutes before we found one with a vacancy. The owner led Charlotte upstairs to inspect the room while I said I'd wait in the street. I was rolling a fresh cigarette when I heard a scooter come to a stop behind me. I was half-turning in its direction when the passenger launched himself from behind the driver and hit me with what looked like a broken chair-leg. It connected with one of my temples and sent me to my knees. A hand was rummaging in my pockets. It pulled out the notes from the till and rubbed them in my face. Then another smack on the side of the head and Harry climbed back aboard, the driver revving the small engine hard as they fled the scene. Pedestrians had stopped to gawp, but only for a moment. There were no offers of help as I scrabbled to pick up my pouch of tobacco. I got to my feet

'You know who did this?'

'I didn't pay him for the drugs.'

Her eyes hardened. 'Say that again.' And when I didn't, she just nodded slowly, as if a small lump of dope explained everything. She clasped me by one wrist. 'Come upstairs. We need to wash that clean.'

I resisted long enough to finish the cigarette, then allowed myself to be led up a dark twisting stairwell to her room. It was tiny and stifling, the window open and shutters closed in a vain attempt to keep out the afternoon heat. Charlotte's rucksack lay on the bed. She moved it and made me sit down, there being no chair. Then she knelt in front of me, examining the damage.

'It's deep,' she said. There was a thin towel on the end of the bed and she took it with her when she left the room. I could hear water running in the sink of the communal bathroom along the hall. Then she was back, dabbing and wiping.

'Any nausea?' she asked.

'No more than usual.'

She smiled as if I'd made a joke. 'You're being very brave,' she cooed.

'I'm tougher than you think.'

'I'm sure you are.' She made another trip to the bathroom to rinse the towel. This time she wiped it slowly across all of my face, studying my features as she worked. 'You're filthy, Ronald. Really you need a bath.'

'Will you scrub my back?'

'I might.' Her eyes were locked on mine. I leaned forwards and kissed her on the mouth.

'You're bristly,' she said afterwards. 'But I sort of like it.'

So I kissed her again. Then we were standing, arms wrapped around one another. My hands felt beneath her sweat-dampened blouse, running down her spine. Our mouths opened as our tongues got to work, and she gave a small moan. Her fingers brushed the front of my trousers, then started to work at the zip. My eyes were still open but hers were closed, as she concentrated hard on fulfilling the whole purpose of the trip. So greedy and so intent on her own selfish self. I put my hand on hers, squeezing. She opened her eyes.

'I'm going to take that bath,' I said.

'Good idea,' she replied, sounding only half-convinced. 'There's only the one towel though, and it's already wet.'

'I'll be fine.' I gave a smile and a wink and managed to escape the airless room. The bath was old and stained but hot water gushed from its tap. I locked the door before stripping. There were bruises on my body I was at a loss to explain. Piled on the floor, my clothes looked like rags. I sank into the water and slid beneath its surface. I had been soaking only a couple of minutes when Charlotte tried the door.

'I won't be long,' I called out.

'I thought you wanted someone to scrub your back.'

'Another time.'

I could sense her lingering. But she moved away eventually, her bedroom door closing. I was debating my next move. Get dressed and slink away? Would that make me a coward? No, I would talk to her face-to-face and explain everything. I would tell her about Benjamin Turk and Alice and my newly blossoming life. We would part as friends, and I would then pay a visit to Harry and Mike, where both men would learn what happened to people who crossed me.

'Yes,' I said to the bathroom walls, nodding slowly to myself.

And then I closed my eyes and slid below the waterline again.

The water had turned tepid by the time I climbed out. I used the towel as best I could, and slid back into my clinging clothes. Blood still trickled from the cut, so I held the towel as a compress as I unlocked the door and padded down the hall. The door to Charlotte's room stood gaping. Charlotte herself lay on the bed, half-undressed and with a scarf knotted tightly around her neck, digging into the flesh. Her eyes and tongue bulged, her face almost purple. I knew she was dead, and knew, too, the identity of the culprit. She had unpacked one dress from her rucksack, the one almost identical to Alice's. Pushing open the shutters, I looked down on to the courtyard and saw a familiar flash of colour. Alice was heading for the street.

I studied Charlotte a final time, knowing there was nothing to be done, then ran to the stairs, barging past the hotelier, who was on the way up. I crossed the courtyard, scanning the pavement to left and right. Making a decision, I started running again. I didn't know Alice's address or even her surname. Would she head for the Seine and the derelicts we had shared our wine with? Or to the bookshop, where she could wait for me on my infested alcove bed? Bars and cafés and the usual landmarks... We had criss-crossed the city, making it our own.

But there was only one destination I could think of – Turk's apartment.

She wasn't outside, nor was she seated on the stairs. I climbed to the top floor and tried the door – locked, as before. But this time when I hit it with my fist, there were sounds from inside. Benjamin Turk opened the door and studied me from head to foot.

'It looks to me as though you're finally ready,' he said with a thin smile, ushering me in.

'Have you seen Alice?' I demanded.

'Forget about her,' he said, his back to me as he hobbled towards the living-room. 'I've laid everything out for you.' He was pointing towards the desk. Various documents lay there. 'Took me some time and effort, but you'll only begin to comprehend when you examine them.'

'What are they?'

'The story of Edwin Hythe. Sit down. Read. I'll fetch you a drink.'

'I don't want a drink.' But I realised that I did – I wanted the darkest wine in the largest glass imaginable. Turk seemed to understand this, and returned with a glass filled almost to the brim. I gulped it down, exhaling only afterwards.

'Does the wound hurt?' he was asking.

I dabbed at my head. 'No,' I said.

'Then you should read.' He pulled over a chair so he could sit next to me, and while

I focused on the various sheets of paper he explained the significance.

'Stevenson and Hythe were close friends as students, belonging to the same clubs and drinking in the same low dives late into the night. Then the murder of a prostitute is recorded in the newspaper and there's a parting. Hythe disappears from Stevenson's life. The murderer is never apprehended. When Stevenson writes a novel about just such a woman, his wife persuades him it is not going to be good for his reputation. But Hythe, too, hears about it, and makes his way to Bournemouth. He comes from money so he stays at the best hotel in town, a hotel that keeps impeccable records.' He tapped the photocopied sheet showing Hythe's signature in the guest book, along with the duration of his stay. 'It's fairly obvious that Hythe was the killer and that Stevenson was either a witness or else was privy to his friend's confession. The golden young man Stevenson had known in Edinburgh was by now a dissolute figure, in trouble with creditors, disowned by his family, earning a living of sorts from any number of illegal activities.' He tapped a series of court reports and newspaper stories. 'Pimping, trafficking, receiving stolen goods... And with a temper on him. One arrest talks of the superhuman rage of the man after too much drink had been taken.' Turk paused. 'And when Hythe left Bournemouth, Stevenson sat down and wrote *Jekyll and Hyde* in three days. Not the version we know, but one set in Edinburgh, where Hythe aka Hyde attacks and kills a harlot rather than trampling a child. Again, he was dissuaded from publishing it. Fanny knew what it would mean – people in Edinburgh would talk. They would remember the killing of the prostitute. They would know

George about you and decided it was no mere coincidence. Which is why I asked him to send you on that particular errand.'

'I don't understand.'

'It's on your mother's side,' he said, running a finger back up the family tree from my name. 'You are descended from Edwin Hythe. His blood in your blood, and with it, unfortunately, his curse.'

'His what?' I was rubbing at my eyes, trying to blink them into some kind of focus.

'Your devil has been long caged, Ronald. He has come out *roaring*!'

There was a mad gleam in his eye as he spoke. I leapt to my feet. 'You're crazy,' I told him. '*You're* the devil here! You and your damned Alice!'

'There is no Alice.'

'She knows you – she runs errands…'

But he was shaking his head. 'There's only

you, Ronald. You and the demon that's been sleeping deep inside you, waiting for the right catalyst. Paris is that catalyst.'

'Where are the manuscripts?' I demand ed, looking about me. 'The two unpublished novels?'

He gave a shrug. 'You've seen all there is. Nothing more than fragments.'

'You're lying!'

'Believe what you will.'

'Alice is *real*!'

He was chuckling as he shook his head again. His silver-topped walking-stick glinted at me from its resting-place by the desk. I grabbed it and raised it over my head. Rather than shrink from me in fear, his smile seemed to widen. I bared my teeth and struck him across the side of the head. He staggered but stayed on his feet, so I hit him again. He wheeled away from me into the long hallway. I stayed a few footsteps behind him as I continued to rain down blows upon his head and back until he fell, just inside the front door. He was still conscious, but his breathing was ragged, blood bubbling from his mouth. A few more blows and he lay still. I hauled him by his feet away from the door so I could open it and make my escape.

Outside, I could hear sirens. Police cars, probably, heading for a hotel not too far away, where passers-by would be able to describe the bloodied figure running from the scene. Alice was standing on the opposite pavement, her eyes full of understanding. We shared a smile before I looked to left and right. There was plenty of traffic, but I started to cross towards her, knowing it would stop for me. When I looked again, however, she had vanished. Pedestrians and drivers were beginning to stare. I noted the fresh spattering of bright

Death Sentences

SHORT STORIES TO DIE FOR

A collection of original short stories
about deadly books from the world's
best crime writers.

'What treats you have in store... all these stories
show their authors to be masters of their craft'
Ian Rankin

Find out more at
www.bookgrail.com/store/death-sentences